THE LIVING AND LEARNING ENCYCLOPEDIA

The Living & Learning Encyclopedia
For Children

A growing, fascinating new series of interesting and amusing information in three categories: Community, Materials and Foods. All crafted in a child-friendly and easy-to-understand language, for kids of all ages.

Trash
Menucha Fuchs

Mail
Menucha Fuchs

Electricity
Menucha Fuchs

Money
Menucha Fuchs

WOOD
Menucha Fuchs

PAPER
Menucha Fuchs

GLASS
Menucha Fuchs

PLASTIC
Menucha Fuchs

Wool
Menucha Fuchs

MILK
Menucha Fuchs

BREAD
Menucha Fuchs

RICE
Menucha Fuchs

SALT
Menucha Fuchs

Coffee
Menucha Fuchs

Citrus
Menucha Fuchs

Eggs
Menucha Fuchs

Tea
Menucha Fuchs

Olives
Menucha Fuchs

Potatoes
Menucha Fuchs

MW00743957

STORYTIME WITH MENUCHA F

with
Menucha Fuchs

Everyone Has a Place

2 Menucha Fuchs
Fish Without Taste

3 Menucha Fuchs
An Olive from the House

4 Menucha Fuchs
The Band

5 Menucha Fuchs
Doctor Pretend

6 Menucha Fuchs
To Fly Like a Bird

7 Menucha Fuchs
The Brave Boy

MASHAL V'NIMSHAL

Who Does the King Love Best?

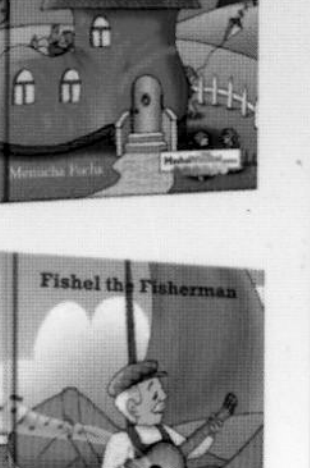
And the Winner Is...
Fishel the Fisherman
Menucha Fuchs

King of the Animals

Fish Without Taste

Nathan went to the sea.
Today he was a fisherman.
He had a net, a fishing rod,
and lots of yummy treats.

Nathan called out,
"Little fish, little fish!
Come to Nathan, fast!"
But no fish came.

Nathan opened his bag and took out a whole bar of milk chocolate.

He tied the chocolate to the hook,
threw it into the sea, and waited.

Nathan called out,
"Little fish, little fish!
Come to Nathan, fast!"
But no fish came.

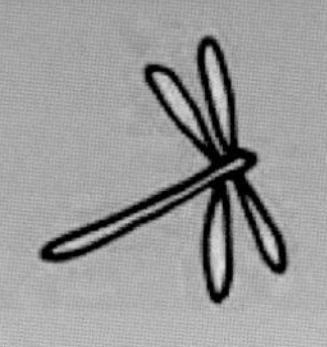

Nathan pulled back his rod and opened his bag. What did he find? A lollipop! He tied the lollipop to the hook, threw it into the sea, and waited calmly.

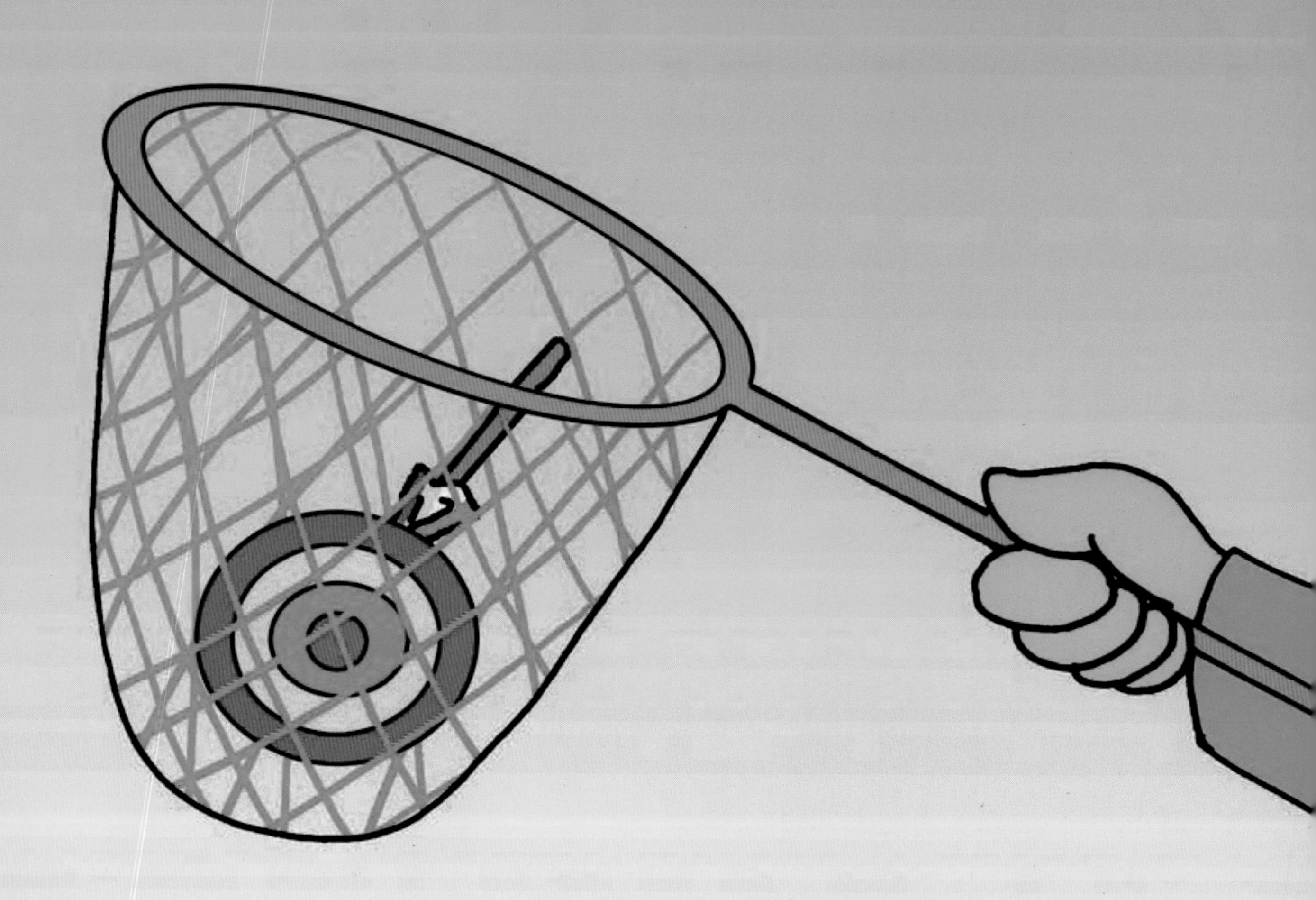

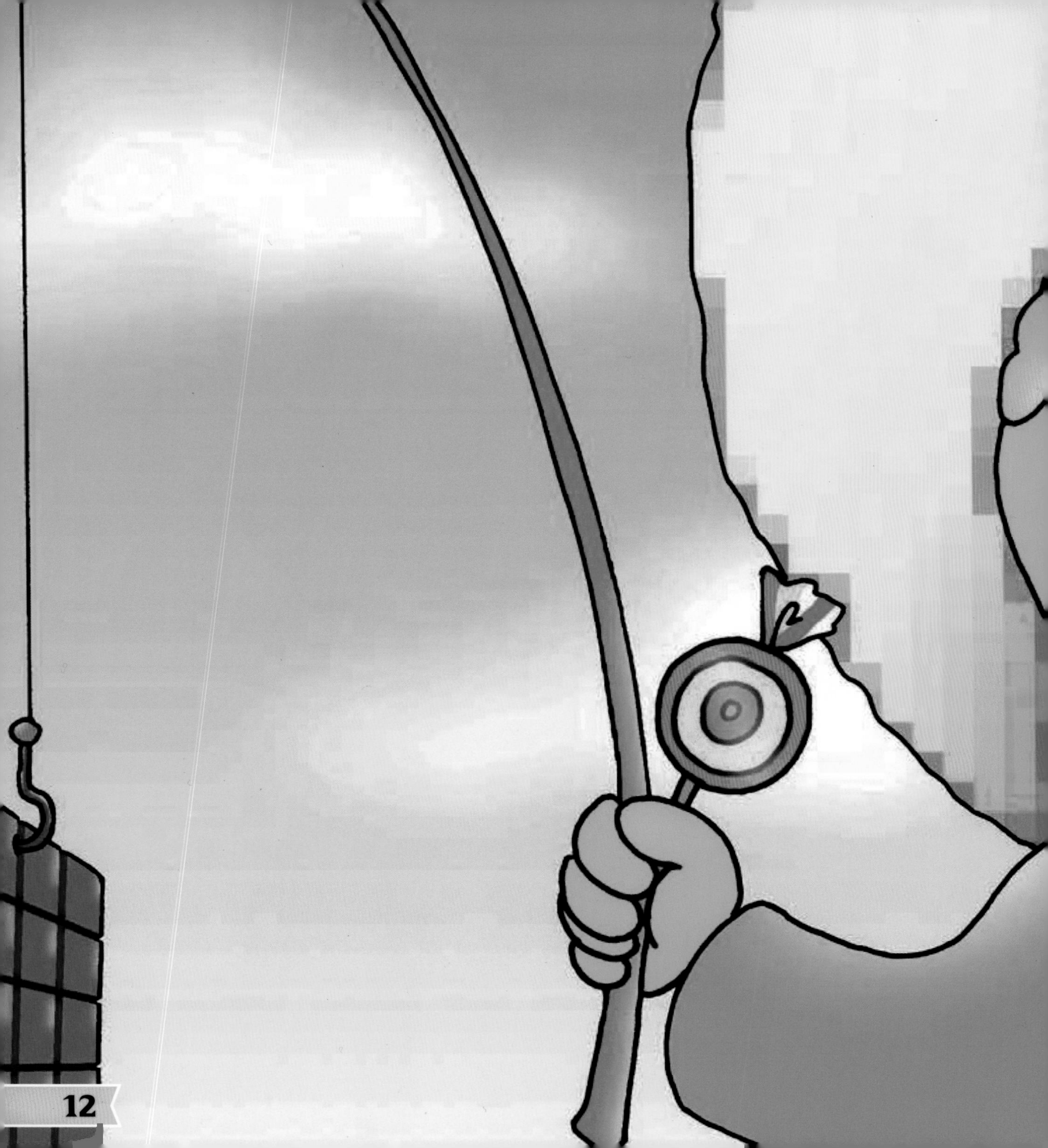

Nathan called out,
"Little fish, little fish!
Come to Nathan, fast!"
But no fish came.

Nathan saw a real fisherman catching fish with his rod. “Mr. Fisherman,” said Nathan, “how do you catch the fish?

I gave them my best candy, but they're not coming to me!"

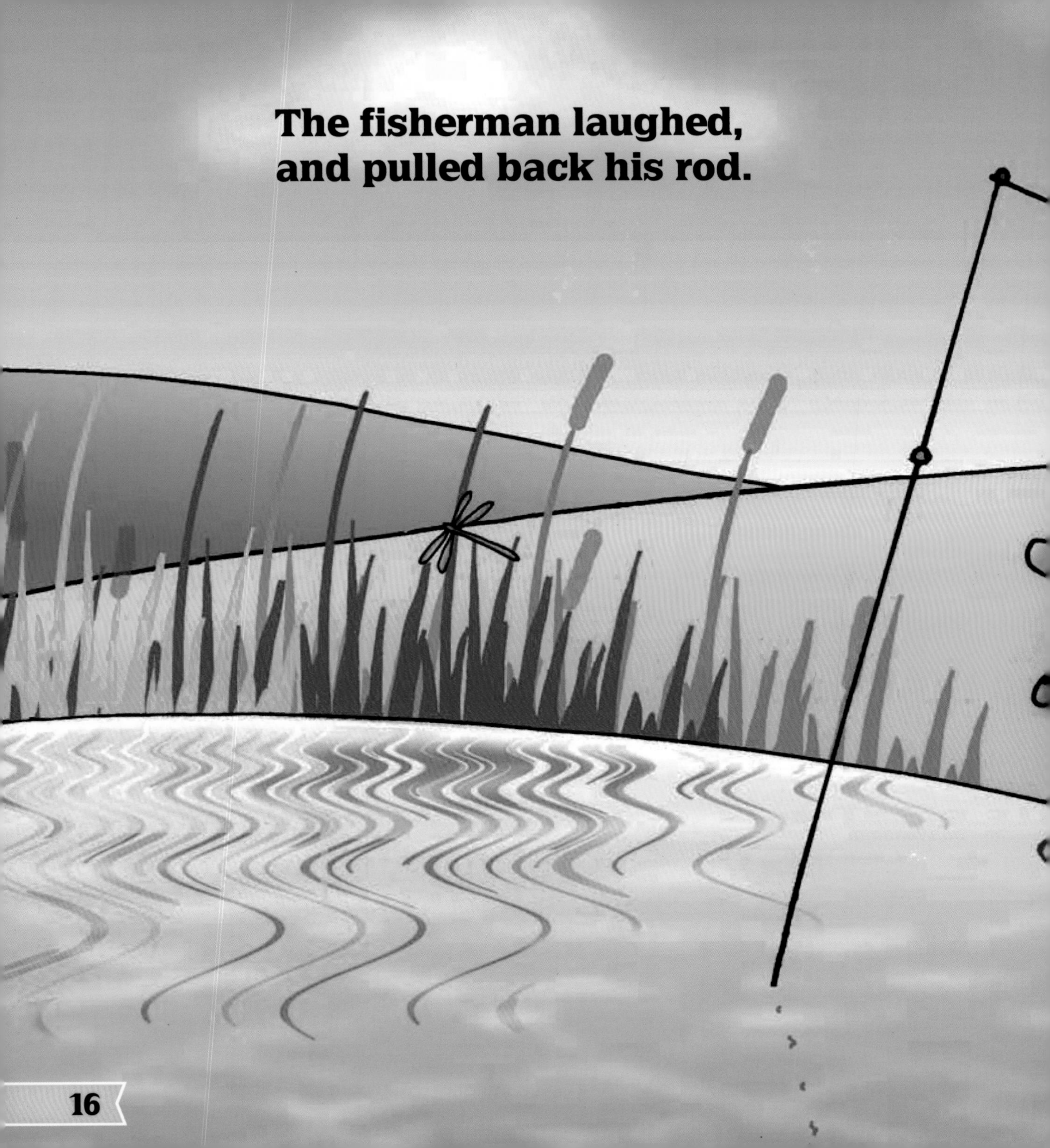

The fisherman laughed,
and pulled back his rod.

Nathan looked at the rod.
What did the fisherman tie to the hook?
Not chocolate, not candy,
just a small piece of bread.

PUTTING EDUCATION, FUN AND
LONG HOURS OF ENTERTAINMENT
INTO YOUR HANDS!

MENUCHA
PUBLISHERS

MORE EXCITING & EDUCATIONAL BOOKS FROM

Menucha Fuchs

ANIMAL KINGDOM

Aviva Ant
Finds Her Food

Baila Butterfly
Learns to Fly

Kalmi Camel
Comes to Town

Libby Ladybug
Learns to Shine

Perry Porcupine
Pops Up

Tully Turtle
Tells His Tale

Penina Penguin
Paddles Through

Wally Wagtail
Wings His Way Home

Solly Snake
Slithers Past

Simi Spider
Scuttles Up

MARVELOUS MOISHY

Marvelous Moishe's
NEW BABY SISTER

Marvelous Moishy
TELLS THE TRUTH

Marvelous Moishy
DRESSES HIMSELF

Marvelous Moishy
ENTERTAINS HIMSELF

Marvelous Moishe's
PACIFIER

Marvelous Moishy
SPEAKS UP

Marvelous Moishy
STAYS AWAY FROM STRANGERS

Marvelous Moishy
LEARNS TO SHARE

Marvelous Moishy
TEACHES MIRI WHAT TO SAY

Marvelous Moishy
LEARNS TO BENTCH

Marvelous Moishy
HELPS HIS MOMMY

LISTENS TO HIS MOMMY

Marvelous Moishy
ISN'T AFRAID
IS SICK

DOESN'T RUN INTO THE STREET

Marvelous Moishy
IS MOVING

ASKS "WHY?"

CAN DO IT BY HIMSELF

DOESN'T CHEAT

EATS HEALTHY FOOD